Katie Woo

Moo, Katie Woo!

by Fran Manushkin

illustrated by Tammie Lyon

Katie Woo is published by Picture Window Books,
1710 Roe Crest Drive
North Mankato, Minnesota 56003
www.capstonepub.com

Text © 2013 Fran Manushkin
Illustrations © 2013 Picture Window Books

Library of Congress Cataloging-in-Publication Data
Manushkin, Fran.
 Moo, Katie Woo! / by Fran Manushkin; illustrated by Tammie Lyon.
p. cm. — (Katie Woo)
 Summary: Katie and her class visit a farm, and find out where eggs and milk come from.
 ISBN 978-1-4048-7653-8 (library binding)
 ISBN 978-1-4048-8047-4 (pbk.)
 1. Woo, Katie (Fictitious character)—Juvenile fiction. 2. Chinese Americans—Juvenile fiction. 3. Farms—Juvenile fiction. 4. School field trips—Juvenile fiction. [1. Chinese Americans—Fiction. 2. Farms—Fiction. 3. School field trips—Fiction.] I. Lyon, Tammie, ill. II. Title. III. Series: Manushkin, Fran. Katie Woo.
 PZ7.M3195Mno 2013
 813.54—dc23   2012029150

Art Director: Kay Fraser
Graphic Designer: Kristi Carlson

Photo Credits:
Greg Holch, pg. 26
Tammie Lyon, pg. 26

Printed in the United States of America in Stevens Point, Wisconsin.

092012
006937WZS13

Table of Contents

Chapter 1
Field Trip 5

Chapter 2
Farm Fun 11

Chapter 3
Lost! 17

Chapter 1
Field Trip

One day, Miss Winkle

asked the class, "Where do

eggs and milk come from?"

"From the store," said

Katie Woo.

"That's true," said Miss

Winkle. "But before that,

they came from chickens

and cows."

"I'd like to see those

chickens and cows," said

Katie.

"Me too," yelled JoJo.

"Me three!" joked Pedro.

"You will," said Miss
Winkle. "Tomorrow we are
going to a farm."

The class rode a bus to the farm. When they got there, Farmer Jordan showed Katie how to milk a cow.

"Moo!" said the cow.

"Moo to you!" joked Katie Woo.

"Now let's visit the chickens," said Miss Winkle. The chicks were cheeping, the roosters were crowing, and the hens were laying eggs.

Pedro joked, "If these
eggs fall down, they will be
scrambled eggs."

"Yuck!" said JoJo. "What
a mess!"

Chapter 2

Farm Fun

Miss Winkle asked Farmer

Jordan, "Where are the

kids?"

Katie laughed. "Miss

Winkle, we are right here!"

"I mean the baby goats,"
said Miss Winkle. "They are
called kids."

"Oh!" said Katie. "I am
learning a lot!"

"These kids are cool!"

said Katie. "They jump and

bounce around just like us!"

"Come and see my fields," said Farmer Jordan. "I'm growing corn for popcorn."

"Yum!" yelled Katie. "I love popcorn! And I'm getting hungry!"

Everybody sat down
for lunch. "I made these
cupcakes," said Katie. "They
have eggs in them."

"Thank you for my eggs,"
Katie called to the chickens.

Katie drank some milk.

"Thank you for my milk,"

she called to the cows.

Chapter 3

Lost!

"It's time to go back to school," said Miss Winkle. "Please line up to walk back to the bus."

"I am still hungry,"

said Katie. "I'd love some

popcorn! The sun is so hot,

the corn should be popping

soon."

Katie walked into the cornfield. "This row of corn is not popping," she said. "I will go to the next row."

"This corn isn't popping either," sighed Katie. "I'd better go back." But the corn was so tall Katie couldn't find her way out!

"Oh, no!" Katie cried. "I'm lost."

Suddenly she heard,

"Moo, Katie Woo! Moo,

Katie Woo!" It was her class

calling her!

Katie followed the sounds

back to her class.

"I'm found!" She smiled.

"Thank you for the moos!"

Katie told Farmer Jordan, "Something is wrong with your corn. It's not popping."

"I know," said Farmer Jordan. "That happens on your stove, not in the field."

"Oh," said Katie. "I know that now!"

On the way home, Katie said, "I would like to be a farmer."

"You just like the moos," teased JoJo.

"I do! I really do!" said Katie Woo.

About the Author

Fran Manushkin is the author of many popular picture books, including *Baby, Come Out!*; *Latkes and Applesauce: A Hanukkah Story*; *The Tushy Book*; *The Belly Book*; and *Big Girl Panties*. There is a real Katie Woo — she's Fran's great-niece — but she never gets in half the trouble of the Katie Woo in the books. Fran writes on her beloved Mac computer in New York City, without the help of her two naughty cats, Chaim and Goldy.

About the Illustrator

Tammie Lyon began her love for drawing at a young age while sitting at the kitchen table with her dad. She continued her love of art and eventually attended the Columbus College of Art and Design, where she earned a bachelors degree in fine art. After a brief career as a professional ballet dancer, she decided to devote herself full time to illustration. Today she lives with her husband, Lee, in Cincinnati, Ohio. Her dogs, Gus and Dudley, keep her company as she works in her studio.

Glossary

bounce (BOUNSS)—to spring back after hitting something

cheeping (CHEEP-ing)—making a high-pitched, chirplike sound

cornfield (KORN-feeld)—a piece of open land used to plant corn

crowing (KROH-ing)—making a loud, crying noise

scrambled (SKRAM-buhld)—mixed up or mixed together

Discussion Questions

1. Have you ever visited a farm? What sorts of things did you see there?

2. If you were a farmer, what animals or crops would you like to raise? Why?

3. Have you ever gotten lost or separated from your parents or guardian? What happened?

Writing Prompts

1. List three things that Katie saw at the farm. Be sure to use complete sentences.

2. Think about the animals Katie saw at the farm. Draw a picture of your favorite one. Then write a sentence or two to explain why it is your favorite.

3. Pretend you are Farmer Jordan and you need to hire a farm helper. Write an advertisement for the paper. List the skills that a farm helper needs.

Popcorn on the Cob

This project takes popcorn and makes it into corn on the cob. All it takes is some colored paper and pretty ribbon! A grown-up will need to help, too! This recipe makes about 10 cobs.

What you need for the popcorn:

- 9 x 13 inch pan, sprayed with cooking spray

- wooden spoon

- 4 quarts popped popcorn, from 1/2 cup unpopped

- 1 to 2 cups small, colorful candies, such as Skittles or M&Ms

- 6 tablespoons butter

- 5 cups mini marshmallows

- cooking spray

What you do:

1. Put popcorn in the baking dish. Mix in the candies.

2. Melt butter in a medium saucepan over low heat. Add the marshmallows and constantly stir with wooden spoon until melted.

3. Pour the marshmallow mix over popcorn mix, and stir to mix evenly.

4. Let cool slightly. Spray your hands with cooking spray, then form the popcorn into corn-cob shapes. Now package them!

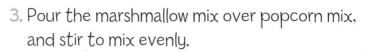

What you need for the package:

- small narrow Baggies with twist ties

- strips of yellow tissue paper, measuring about 6 inches wide and 15 inches long

- strips of green tissue paper, measuring about 8 inches wide and 18 inches long

- 8-inch long pieces of yellow or green ribbon

What you do:

1. Place each corn cob into a Baggie. Secure with a twist tie.

2. Wrap a strip of yellow paper around the Baggie, covering the back but leaving the front showing. Repeat with a strip of green paper.

3. Twist the paper at the top of the Baggie, so that it looks like a cob of corn.

4. Tie a ribbon around the top of your corn cob.

THE FUN DOESN'T STOP HERE!

Discover more at www.capstonekids.com

💜 Videos & Contests

✿ Games & Puzzles

💜 Friends & Favorites

✿ Authors & Illustrators

Find cool websites and more books like this one at www.facthound.com. Just type in the Book ID: **9781404876538** and you're ready to go!